Little Red Riding Hood

 nosy crow

Illustrated by
Ed Bryan

Once upon a time, there was a kind and helpful girl called **Little Red Riding Hood.** She lived with her mother in a cottage at the edge of a forest.

Soon the basket was packed,
and Little Red Riding Hood
was ready to go.

As Little Red Riding Hood was leaving,
her mother gave her a warning.
"Be careful in the forest and beware
of the Big Bad Wolf!" she said.

And Little Red Riding Hood went on her way.

She had not gone very far before
the **Big Bad Wolf** appeared.

"Hello, little girl," said the wolf. "Where are you going?"
"Oh, I'm just walking to my grandma's with this basket
of food," said Little Red Riding Hood, and off she went.

Little Red Riding Hood soon came to a clearing in the forest filled with **lovely flowers**. "How **pretty!**" said Little Red Riding Hood.

She knew that her grandma **loved daisies** so she picked some, and popped them into her basket. Then she continued on her way.

Little Red Riding Hood skipped off through the trees, and before too long she came to a big old **oak tree.**

"Oh, look!" she said.
"What lovely **acorns**!
I'll put those in my basket.
You never know when they
might come in handy."

With the **flowers** and the **acorns**
in her basket, Little Red Riding Hood
continued on her way.

Little Red Riding Hood wandered along
and, by and by, she came across a
bear with a **huge** jar of **honey**.

"Hello," said the bear.
"Can you help me pour this **honey** into
my jars? You can take a jar with you if you do."
So Little Red Riding Hood stopped to help the bear.

Then, with the flowers, the acorns and the honey in her basket, Little Red Riding Hood skipped off through the trees.

In next to no time, Little Red Riding Hood
arrived at her grandma's house.

"Hello Grandma!" she called. "I'm here
with a basket full of all sorts of things!"
"I'm in bed, my dear," called a voice
through the door.

It was quite **dark** inside the cottage.
Little Red Riding Hood went over to the bed
with a **curious** look on her face.

"Oh, Grandma, what **big ears** you have!"
said Little Red Riding Hood.

"All the better to **hear**
you with, my dear . . ."
came the reply.

"Oh, Grandma, what **big eyes** you have!"
said Little Red Riding Hood.

"All the better to **see** you
with, my dear . . ."
came the reply.

"Oh, Grandma, what **big teeth** you have!"
said Little Red Riding Hood.

"**All the better to** . . .

. . . **eat** you with, my dear!"
said the Big Bad Wolf.
He had been disguised
as Grandma all along!

And with that, the wolf **jumped** out of the bed and **chased** Little Red Riding Hood around the room!

Quickly, Little Red Riding Hood **reached** into her basket. She took out the **flowers** and waved them under the wolf's **nose.**

The wolf **sneezed**
and **sneezed**
and **sneezed!**

But **that** didn't
stop him for long.

So Little Red Riding Hood **reached** into her basket **again**. She pulled out the **acorns** and threw them onto the **floor**.

The wolf **skidded**
and **slipped**
and **skated**
all over the floor.

But **that** didn't
stop him either.

So Little Red Riding Hood **reached** into her basket for the very **last** time. She took out the jar of **honey** and threw it **all over** the Big Bad Wolf.

"**Yuck!** I'm covered in **sticky honey!**"
yelped the wolf.

"Just you wait and see
what happens **next!**"
said Little Red
Riding Hood . . .

The sticky honey smelled SO delicious that a swarm of bees flew in through the window and chased the wolf out of the door.

The Big Bad Wolf ran down the road and he was never, **ever** seen again.

As soon as the Big Bad Wolf was **gone**,
Little Red Riding Hood **unlocked**
the cupboard . . .

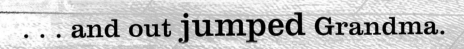

. . . and out **jumped** Grandma.

Little Red Riding Hood laid out the
delicious food from her basket, then she
and her grandma had a wonderful feast.
And they both lived **happily** ever after.